Latkes and Applesauce

A Hanukkah Story

by FRAN MANUSHKIN

Illustrated by ROBIN SPOWART

SCHOLASTIC INC.
New York Toronto London Auckland Sydney

ISBN 0-590-42265-0

12 11 10 9 8   6 7/9

Printed in the U.S.A.   09

Design by Claire Counihan

For my favorite latke lovers,
Esther, Walter, Debbie,
and David Hautzig
– F.M.

To Rabbi David Kopstein
and Patti Philo
– R.S.

O you like to eat latkes and applesauce on Hanukkah? Of course you do. Who but a fool would say no to such a question! Well, here is a story about latkes and applesauce, and perhaps a miracle. Maybe yes, maybe no.

It happened long ago in a village far away, where there lived a little family named Menashe. Papa and Mama Menashe were tailors who had two children, Rebecca and Ezra.

Rebecca and Ezra were wonderful children who helped their mama and papa. Every year when it came time to celebrate Hanukkah, they dug up potatoes to make the latkes, and they picked the apples for applesauce.

But one year, winter came suddenly and snow began to fall – not just a lazy flake or two or a little bit of a flurry. No! This was a tremendous blizzard – as if all heaven's featherbeds had burst!

And when did this furious blizzard begin? Of course—on the first night of Hanukkah!

"Come, sunset is upon us," Papa called to his family. "It's time to light the candles and celebrate the Hanukkah miracle." So Papa sang the blessings and Mama lit the *shammes*, and Rebecca lit the first candle.

"Ah!" they sighed together at the beautiful light. Then Papa set the Hanukkah menorah in the window so all could see its glory.

"Now," declared Papa, "for the next eight days we shall celebrate the miracle of Hanukkah with feasting and gladness. Bring on the latkes and applesauce!"

"Papa," said Mama, "the blizzard has swallowed our feast. All of the potatoes are buried in the snow, and as for apples, this year we had so few."

"No latkes?" gasped Papa, and his bright eyes dimmed. "Ah well, then let us sip our soup."

So, sitting as closely as birds in a nest, Mama and Papa and Rebecca and Ezra sipped their soup together. Then they sang a joyful Hanukkah song with the wind whistling along through the walls.

"*Sssh!*" said Rebecca, suddenly. "I hear someone crying."
Soon they all heard it—a mewing and crying—as if all the sad
spirits in the world were set loose! Rebecca opened the door
a crack, and in walked a wet orange kitten!

"Mew, mew, mew!" the kitten cried.

Rebecca quickly patted her dry with a rag. "Papa," said Rebecca, "the kitten must have seen our candles!"

Mama filled a tiny dish with milk. After the kitten lapped it up, she purred, falling asleep in Rebecca's lap.

"Now, Rebecca," said Papa firmly, "we must return this kitten to her mother."

Rebecca shook her head. "Papa, this kitten hasn't *got* a mother. No mother would let her kitten wander alone in a storm!"

"Yes," agreed Ezra. "That is why the kitten was crying. And since you said we mustn't be sad on Hanukkah, I think we should keep this kitten."

"Sad? A cat?" Papa pulled at his beard.

"A cat is one of God's creatures," declared Mama. "Of course we will care for her."

Rebecca leaped up and hugged her mother. "Mama, what shall we name her?"

"A name should fit as well as a glove," said Papa. "Take care to name her well."

"I will," Rebecca promised, "but right now I want to play dreidel."

The little kitten spun the dreidel so well, she won two nuts and a raisin! And when the candles flickered out, everyone went to bed.